snOwflakes Aren't scared Because...

Written by Emily Samantha Ruth Mikelsons
Illustrated by Laura Nicholson

WestBow Press books may be ordered through booksellers or by contacting:

WestBow Press
A Division of Thomas Nelson
1663 Liberty Drive
Bloomington, IN 47403
www.westbowpress.com
1-(866) 928-1240

Because of the dynamic nature of the Internet, any web addresses or links contained in this book may have changed since publication and may no longer be valid. The views expressed in this work are solely those of the author and do not necessarily reflect the views of the publisher, and the publisher hereby disclaims any responsibility for them.

ISBN: 978-1-4908-0328-9 (sc)
ISBN: 978-1-4908-0329-6 (e)

Library of Congress Control Number: 2013913343

Printed in the United States of America.

WestBow Press rev. date: 08/14/2013

This book is dedicated to my grandpa in the hospital.

If you want to give this book to encourage someone special you can place their name in here:

_____

About the Author

Emily wrote "Snowflakes Aren't Scared Because…" when she was in Grade 2. Her teacher marveled at how beautiful it read and what a deep truth it conveyed. So we as a family decided to get it published. Emily's oldest sister did the illustrations and her oldest brother did the organizing. Emily created the story, did the writing and editing.

Emily is now in Grade 5. She attends a Christian school, plays soccer, loves overnight Christian camp in the summer, and loves music. She preached her first sermon in Grade 4 at her great grandmother's funeral. Emily told the congregation that you can tell if someone is a Christian by how much love they show others.

About the Illustrator

Laura is Emily's oldest sister and illustrated the pictures for "Snowflakes Aren't Scared Because…". She graduated from the University of Waterloo with a degree in Arts and Business, majoring in Studio Fine Arts. In her third and fourth year of study, she focused her body of work on photography. After graduation, she moved on to Wilfrid Laurier University where she received her Bachelor's degree in Education.

Laura now runs her own business as a photographer. Her work and projects can be found at www.lnphotography.ca.

I was sleeping on my cloud.

Suddenly, God wanted us to snow! Fall
had just ended. We had to wake up.

We went to the snow catapult that shot us into the sky.

We started to float down to the ground. We were falling towards a house. The children had just finished lunch and they were playing outside.

The children loved to stick out their tongues and eat us all up. We never wanted to come down, but we had to.

I saw all the children playing outside. There were ten kids wanting to eat us. We got very scared.

I was the biggest snowflake. One boy was aiming to eat me. I felt like I was crash landing in an airplane!

I got closer and closer to the boy's mouth.
He was so close to eating me. Then the
most wonderful thing happened!

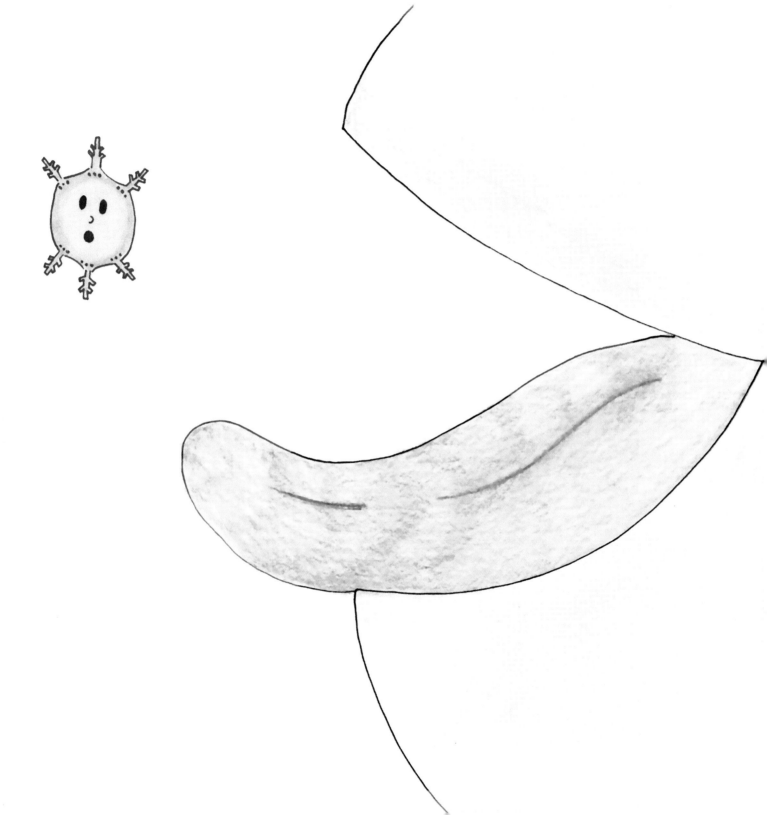

Someone else caught me just before I floated into his mouth! She was a girl. I was too shocked to melt in her hand. She put me in a cold glass jar.

After she had her dinner she took me outside
and put me safely on the ground.

At the end of winter God brought us back up
to the clouds so we could rest. Then God said,
"Next winter you are going to do the same thing,
and I will be with you wherever you go."

Always remember that God is with you wherever you go—even when you are scared.

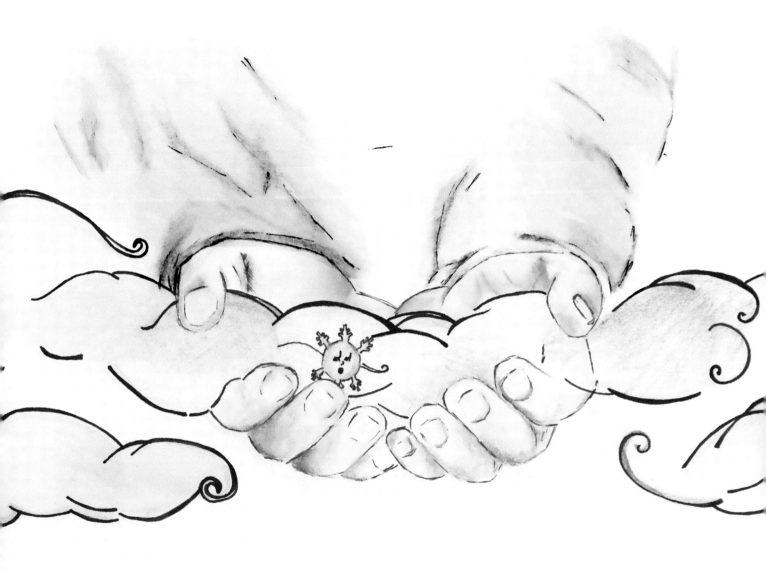

CPSIA information can be obtained
at www.ICGtesting.com
Printed in the USA
LVIC04n1230180913
352981LV00002B

9781490803289